This is the story of two friends: Makareta (Maka for short) and Matz. When the stupid giant Tikitipua stops the world, a goblin maki, also called a tarsier comes flying. These makis are small, cute monkeys with big eyes that live on trees in Asia. Maka and Matz now want to bring the little goblin back to his home country. On their journey, they meet many people and animals. So they also experience some adventures.

Have fun reading!

This book is available as paperback and eBook at Amazon.com. Editions in the following languages are also available: French, German, Portuguese, Spanish, as well as the bilingual versions German/Spanish and German/Portuguese.
The story is also suitable for all readers who want to improve their English.

We have used Font 14 for a better reading experience for children.

Maka, Matz and Maki

by Sven-Ole Andersen

translated by
Dana Deal

Dana lives in Jacksonville, FL.
She works at a university, there, and teaches German.
After receiving an MA in German studies in the U.S., she studied at the University of Salzburg, Austria. Since she enjoys sharing her knowledge of German language and culture, she happily translated this story from the German original.

Illustrations: **Jennifer Pérez**
Jennifer studies at the University of Puerto Rico, campus Rio Piedras.

Translation support: **Andrea M. Acevedo Márquez**, Las Piedras, PR.

Special Thanks to **Paul Bayman**, Ph.D. for his incredible insight and suggestions. Paul is a biologist at The University of Puerto Rico (UPR).
In case you encounter any inconsistencies or controversial issues in the story, do not blame him, blame me, the author. I had to develop a story that is not too scientifically told.

German original:

“Maka, Matz und Maki”

Manuscript review: Dr. Rainer Schnoor
Editor: Hans Markert

12 11 10 9 8 7 6 5 4 3 2 1

ElHeiLi Siduri Publications

Maka and Matz rescue a kiwi egg

Oh, what a beautiful country New Zealand is. There are beautiful landscapes, nice people, clean air, and many sheep. Also, there is an animal that only exists there, the kiwi. A kiwi is a bird that can't fly and has a long curved beak. New Zealand is also home to the Maori, the natives of the country. They live with nature and try not to destroy it. Makareta and her family belong to the Maori people.

Maka

Makareta had long black hair, a button nose, and was able to talk to animals. All those who knew her, simply called her Maka. She usually wore a leather ribbon around her neck that her father had given her with an attached dangling pendant. She always carried a small leather bag, which contained her most important treasures. Sometimes she wore a headband with Maori motifs. Maka and her family had lived in town for a long time, but they had never really felt comfortable there. That's why the family moved back to the countryside and ran a small farm.

Maka's best friend was Matz, a redheaded boy. He too, lived down in the valley and enjoyed bicycling, swimming and sailing. His family also owned a farm and raised sheep. Matz had a pet, of course, a miniature sheep, called Muffy.

Muffy had long white fluffy fur and was sometimes quite stubborn, especially when the children went swimming or sailing. Muffy never wanted to swim because he was afraid of water.

Yesterday was another beautiful day with the sun shining, birds chirping, and sheep bleating. Besides that, it wasn't too hot. Maka had just arrived home from school and made herself comfortable outside on a blanket in the meadow. She wanted to rest before her homework. She hoped to eventually be able to travel to far-away countries and to get to know the people and animals there. Africa, America, Asia, Europe, the Arctic, and even Antarctica - she wanted to go everywhere. She had never even been to Australia, which is the closest country to New Zealand. She wanted to be a veterinarian, that was her big wish.

As she lay in the grass, she fell asleep and began to dream. In her dream, the good fairy Hine appeared and told her that she was smart, beautiful, and that she would have many adventures in the future. It's the kind of dream you'd never want to wake up from.

However, when Maka was having this really nice dream, the earth suddenly shook as if someone stomped with giant steps and whirled everything into the air. Boom, boom, boom. She was lifted somewhat into the air. And again, the earth boomed: Boom, boom, boom. Maka woke up and she was suddenly wide awake. “What was that,” she thought, “an earthquake?” But the quake was much too weak, and even after a short time, it was over again.

She continued to lay on her blanket, still a little frightened. She had her hands crossed under her head and looked dreamily into the bright blue sky. She knew that if you really believed in something and that if you were well prepared for it, then the wish would come true. “That's what the fairy once told her in her dreams,” she believed. After a while, she saw something run past her blanket. It was a kiwi. "Hello, Mr. Kiwi," she said. "Hello, Maka," the bird replied grumpily and kept poking his long beak along the ground. Something was wrong, she thought and asked, "Is everything all right, Mr. Kiwi?"

"Oh," he replied quickly, "I'm just looking for a bite to eat. But I have to hurry. My wife's not in the nest either, and our egg is lying in it unprotected."

Maka knew immediately that the kiwi needed help. In New Zealand, there were not many of its kind anymore. Hence, people helped the kiwis and often took their eggs to a station where they placed them in a device called an incubator. An incubator looks like a giant box and it is pretty warm inside, so that baby birds or other small animals can hatch. When the young were hatched, they were released back into the wild after a short time. If the egg lay unprotected in the nest, another animal could find it and simply eat it. "Mr. Kiwi, I'll call my friend Matz, and then we'll take the egg to the hatchery," Maka called, jumped up, and ran into the house. "Good, good. Thank you very much," the kiwi replied nasally.

As soon as Maka was in the house, she reached for her father's phone and called her friend, Matz. "Matz, you must come quickly," she shouted excitedly into the phone, "Mr. Kiwi and his wife have an egg in their nest. It would be good if we could take care of it and take it to the hatchery. Can you help me?" "Sure," Matz exclaimed into his phone, "I'll be there as soon as I can. Shall I bring Muffy?" "Yes, but hurry," Maka answered quickly and hung up. Matz was immediately very excited.

"Muffy, where are you?" he shouted loudly and ran out to the yard to find his mini-sheep. But Muffy had something better to do and was pretty annoyed. He was licking salt. After all, sheep like salt licking better than anything else. The little white sheep stood in the corner and slobbered on a salty stone. When Matz came closer, Muffy just moaned and grumbled. "Oh, what's the matter? I'm licking this stone right now and I am not in the mood to do anything else." Matz was excited. "Come with me! We need your help. We need you. I'll explain later. Now is no time to lick the

stone," he yelled in an excited voice. "All right. If I *have to*," Muffy said grumpily as he wanted to take one last lick of the salty stone. Just as he was sticking out his tongue, Matz grabbed his fur and lifted him up. With a strong grip, he put Muffy into the basket that hung on the handlebars of his bike. In the basket lay a soft cushion so that the mini sheep was always comfortable when Matz took him along. Muffy lifted his fluffy head out of the basket, looked at him, and shouted: "We are not going to the beach, right?
I don't feel like it at all."

"Be quiet now," Matz said, as he got in a hectic mode. Then he put on his bicycle helmet. When he closed the buckle of his helmet, he also brought out a small helmet for Muffy. "You can't be serious," Muffy bleated. "Safety before beauty. We need you for a rescue operation, Muffy," Matz said and put a mini helmet on the little sheep. Actually, a sheep in a helmet looks pretty silly, but it was safer to wear a helmet to drive through the forest. Muffy made a funny noise, closed his mouth, and kept quiet. Matz got on his bike, and they started riding.

On his way to Maka, he suddenly noticed that his bike had been lifted a few inches up into the air. He heard sounds as if big branches were cracking and the earth was shaking: boom, boom, boom. Muffy also swirled back and forth and almost fell out of his basket. The helmet slid several times over the eyes of the small sheep so that he could not see anything. He was rudely shaken. "Maaaaaa, take it easy," Muffy shouted, "can't you just go straight ahead and be careful?" Matz pulled both brakes and stopped. What was that? Was that really an earthquake? No, the quake was too weak for that. It was like someone was stomping through the forest. Boom, boom, boom.

He looked around several times. But then, there was complete silence, nothing trembled anymore. Everything was quiet. What could that have been? It didn't matter. He jumped back onto his bike and pressed the pedals. Now it was important to act quickly. The kiwi egg must be saved! As he pedaled, sweat came out of all his pores, but he concentrated on the path through the forest.

He was so focused that he did not see the hole in the ground and fell right into it. The wheel overturned, and he and Muffy were thrown to the ground. For a few seconds, there was an eerie silence. Everything was quiet, and both lay almost motionless on the ground. Then Muffy bleated. In his helmet, there was now a big bump on his head because he had fallen on a branch. "Maaaaaa. Did you have to do that? Can't you be more careful?" Matz himself was completely shaken up. After briefly being shocked, he carefully checked for any injuries.

He was lucky, and Muffy wasn't hurt either. First, he checked his bike and put his mini-sheep back into the dented basket. For the rest of the trip, he slowed down a little while Muffy complained all the way.

Maka's house was only a short distance away. Matz had already seen her standing in front of the house waving excitedly. She ran a few yards towards them. He pedaled hard and then braked sharply in front of Maka so that his rear wheel pushed forward sideways.

"There you are, finally," Maka shouted excitedly. At the same time, Muffy shook himself and was glad that they had finally reached their destination. "Yes, we hurried," Matz said. He was still out of breath.

"Hello Maka, phew, I'm sweating. Hongi first," he said. Hongi is the traditional Maori greeting in New Zealand.

To perform it, one presses their forehead and nose against each other. Maka and Matz performed a Hongi every time they met. "Let's go," Maka shouted and quickly gave the mini-sheep a Hongi in his bicycle basket. Muffy grimaced and mumbled a short "Hello."

Then, Matz wanted to know what to do. Maka could hardly hold on, she spoke very quickly, and her voice almost somersaulted while speaking. She told him that Mr. Kiwi was looking for his wife. He was looking for her, while their egg was lying in the nest all alone and without observation. "We must help them, and we must save the egg by bringing it to the hatchery," she said excitedly. Matz surely knew that Maka was right and that they should not waste any time.

"Let’s go," he shouted, "let's save the egg. Hopefully, it’s not too late". Maka froze and turned all white in her face because she was afraid that it might be too late. The tip of her button nose turned red, and she was now even more excited. Matz pushed his bike to the house and leaned it against the wall. Then he lifted Muffy out of the basket, and the children ran off while he held the little sheep in his arms.

They ran into a clearing in the woods near the house. There was a burrow somewhere with Ms. and Mr. Kiwi's nest. Even before they reached the clearing, they heard various sounds.

There was something angrily growling as if someone was getting very upset. At first, however, they only saw Mr. Kiwi standing on the edge. He looked very sad. "What happened, Mr. Kiwi?" Maka asked. The kiwi pointed with its long, curved beak towards the edge of the forest. At first, they saw nothing, but then they discovered how a weasel tried breaking open and devouring the kiwi family's big egg.

Indeed, weasels look cute. They have a soft coat, which is sometimes brown and white, sometimes completely white. They're not very big, but this weasel tried to roll the Kiwis' egg out of the nest, break it open, and then eat it. The children understood immediately. Now the weasel discovered Maka and Matz and wanted to defend its prey. It went wild and hissed angrily.

Maka and Matz were not frightened. They grabbed stones, sticks, and ran towards the egg thief. They screamed as loud as they could. The wild weasel got aggressive and wanted to attack, but then it saw how serious the children were. They screamed so loud that the agile weasel was terrified and ran away. The egg rolled back into the burrow.

Then, something happened that no one had expected. There was again a short and violent quake, during which everyone was thrown into the air in the clearing. After they fell back to the ground again, Maka and Matz looked at each other in surprise. What just happened? Even the wild weasel didn't know what happened. It jumped up, shook itself, and panicked a little bit. Then it ran away as fast as it could.

Maka and Matz ran to the Kiwis' small burrow. They quickly started digging to find the egg. In the meantime, Mr. Kiwi picked himself up and ran to the two children as quickly as he could.

But then he sadly stood nearby and watched them dig and dig. "There!" Matz shouted, "There it is. We got it!" Very slowly and carefully, he laid the egg down, and the shell emerged under a layer of earth. He carefully pushed the sand to the side, so that the egg's shell could not be damaged. Mr. Kiwi watched the action and was suddenly very grateful. "Mr. Kiwi, we'll make it," Maka said and saw tears in the bird's eyes. Then Matz held the kiwi egg in his hand. Suddenly Muffy came walking.

The mini-sheep still had his little helmet on his head and still looked pretty silly. But the helmet had already protected the sheep twice. Like everyone else, Muffy was perplexed because the egg was so huge. After all, a kiwi egg is five times bigger than a chicken egg. Then the sheep went on to complain. "Nobody thinks about me," he bleated.

"Now comes your task, my little sheep," said Matz, "you must help us bring the egg to the hatchery." Muffy looked puzzled again because he did not understand what was going on. Then Matz took the kiwi egg and stowed it safely in Muffy's thick fur. There the egg laid softly and could not be destroyed. Besides, sheepskin is really nice and warm. So the three set off. They ran quickly, but not too fast so that they didn't destroy the egg. Behind them ran the excited Mr. Kiwi with his head bowed. But now he had little hope that his offspring inside the egg was still healthy. Everybody could notice that he was very sad.

The small group silently covered a few miles through the forest before reaching the hatchery. While running, Maka called the hatchery with her cell phone so that the staff could prepare for their arrival. Only Muffy didn't really know what was going on, and as always, he was pretty grumpy. After Maka informed the hatchery, she explained to the sheep what would happen.

They were not allowed to run too fast; to not damage the egg in the sheep’s fur. The staff was already waiting for them in the hatchery, she explained. They would carefully put the egg in an incubator. It is very warm inside the incubator, and an egg can be hatched this way. After a while, Mr. and Ms. Kiwi's little baby would hatch. Kiwis are endangered, and there are not many remaining of these shy birds. That's why all New Zealanders should help bring Kiwi eggs to hatcheries if they find one. Muffy understood everything but was still grumpy. Mr. Kiwi ran behind the small group. He was still sad and wondering where his wife was. But he still had some hope of finding her.

At the same time, the group was on their way to the hatchery, Mr. Kiwi's wife was walking through the forest. She was excited too. She had been searching for food, and by the time she got to the nest, the egg had disappeared. Ms. Kiwi was upset. What had happened? First, she called out loud for Mr. Kiwi.

Then she began to tremble and began to look for their egg in the forest. She didn't know where it was. Her eyes were full of tears, and she sobbed as she kept looking for the egg and desperately kept searching for her husband. After a while in the forest, so far away from the nest, she was exhausted and had to sit. She began to cry terribly. Finally, she gained courage and pulled herself together and started making her way back to the nest.

Meanwhile, Maka, Matz, Muffy with the egg in his fur, and Mr. Kiwi had reached the hatchery. In front of the house stood one of the gamekeepers, who was responsible for a huge area. "Hello, Mr. Ranger!" Matz called when they reached the station. "Hello everyone," he replied, holding his hand as a greeting on his big yellow hat. He was wearing a green uniform and a light blue vest over it. Smiling, he said: "You did that well! Where is the patient?" Everyone was pointing at Muffy. The sheep stood there a little grumpy and remained silent.

At first, the park ranger did not understand, but then Maka and Matz both grabbed the sheep's fur and carefully brought out the large kiwi egg. Now the man understood and rejoiced: "Kids, you are fantastic. You're heroes!" Very slowly, he took the egg from their hands and carried it into the house. Mr. Kiwi watched the whole scene with a sad face, and then the children followed the gamekeeper into the house. Some of his colleagues had prepared everything.

The egg was carefully placed in a yellow box with a small window, then the gamekeeper closed the box and pressed a button. "What happens now? What is this box? What about Mr. Kiwi's egg," Maka asked, and her voice cracked with excitement. "Slow down," said the gamekeeper, explaining to the children and Muffy what was about to happen: "This box is an incubator. Now the egg of the Kiwi family is safe in it. We always watch the egg. It's very warm in the box. It's good for the little one in the egg. It takes a little more heat before it can hatch out of the egg.

We must watch it from now on and hope that it is born healthy." With big eyes, the children looked through the small glass pane of the incubator and saw the egg of the Kiwi family lying inside. It was fascinating for them and they were proud that they had done everything to help the Kiwi family. Now they could only hope and believe that the young one inside the egg was still healthy and would soon hatch out of the egg. They knew that the gamekeepers were experts. So there was a good chance for the little one.

In the small room, it was now very quiet. Then the gamekeeper suddenly said, "You know what? You all should get something to drink, and I'll call Maka's father to have him pick you all up." "Yay," Maka and Matz both shouted, and Muffy made a funny sound. Then everyone looked at sad Mr. Kiwi, standing there all alone in the corner of the room. Everybody felt sorry for him. "Mr. Ranger, can't we take Mr. Kiwi to the nest, and Maka's father will pick us up from there?" Matz asked. He nodded his head and said

calmly: "Good idea. You guys can get going, and I'll call him. I will tell him to pick you up from there."
At that moment, one of his co-workers came in and brought something to drink. It was a wonderful refreshment for everyone. Then Maka and Matz took a last look at the egg in the yellow incubator, bid farewell to the gamekeepers, and set off to take Mr. Kiwi home.

The small group wandered slowly and silently through the forest. On the long march, they met almost all the animals that lived in the forest. They told them about their afternoon adventure. The animals also became very sad and hugged Mr. Kiwi. Everyone wished him good luck. "Never give up hope, Mr. Kiwi!" they always shouted upon farewell.
But Mr. Kiwi couldn't be happy because he didn't know what would happen to the egg. He didn't even know where his wife was. The small group continued to march on. They didn't have a map, but they knew about where they were. They could orient themselves on the position of the sun. Matz also had his compass

with him. After school, he often went hiking and knew that it was important never to get lost. Especially in the great outdoors, you need a compass if you walk for a long time through a terrain you don't know.

Suddenly it returned: that thunder, as if someone was stomping terribly loud. Maka and Matz looked at each other only briefly with big eyes, then the four were whirled a little bit through the air. When the short quake was over, the children just shook their heads. "I've experienced this before today," Maka said. "Me too," Matz replied, "we've been shaken up today already, haven't we, Muffy?" "You could say that," said Muffy and looking puzzled. Mr. Kiwi didn't say anything, he just stood there sadly. Since nothing else happened, the group set off again on the path through the forest.

It was already dark when they finally got to the clearing where Mr. and Ms. Kiwi lived. Exhausted, they looked around. The moonlight fell on the clearing, and all around, it was very quiet, almost incredibly too quiet. Only from somewhere came a soft sobbing as if someone was crying. Muffy discovered a somewhat rounded shadow on the other side of the clearing and was frightened because he thought it was a ghost.

But Mr. Kiwi knew immediately who this shadow belonged to and ran in its direction. Shortly afterward, Maka, Matz, and Muffy heard a sound. The shadow was Ms. Kiwi's. She stood alone in front of her nest for a long time and thought someone had stolen their egg. Mr. and Ms. Kiwi stood together. Sometimes they'd lean against each other. A little further away stood the children and the sheep. They watched them. It made all three sad to see the two birds like this. But sometimes it's better not to say anything, just to keep quiet. They could show the two kiwis that they thought of them and would be there in an emergency.

After a long time, they calmed down and began to tell each other what had happened and what they had done. Ms. Kiwi was a little better now because she knew that there was hope for their egg.

A little later, everyone heard the sound of an engine. Shortly afterward, the clearing was illuminated by spotlights. It was Maka's father's big car, an SUV. He had come to pick up his daughter, Matz, and the sheep. When he got out of the car, he hugged everyone and let them tell him everything. Then he encouraged Mr. and Ms. Kiwi, "You know, it's only natural that you're sad," he told them, "but you also know that your egg is in good hands. The gamekeepers will do everything they can to ensure that your young will hatch soon." They just nodded. "You must be there for each other now. This is a difficult time, but you must not give up hope."

Then he looked at Maka and Matz and said: "Let’s go, children, get in the car, it's late!" Matz took Muffy in his arms and sat down with the sheep in the back seat, while Maka entered the seat next to the driver’s. As a farewell, they waved goodbye to the two kiwis, while the father turned the SUV around and drove slowly out of the clearing. Mr. and Ms. Kiwi stood together and looked silently for a long time in the direction of the taillights as they slowly disappeared into the distance. They still had hope that their little one would hatch out of the egg.

The fairy Hine explains the world

It had been a very exhausting day for everyone. First, Maka's father took Matz home and brought his bicycle and Muffy. Then, he rushed off in the car with his daughter. Maka was so tired that she fell asleep in the passenger seat. Matz was also really tired, but he checked again if all his animals were well looked after for the night.

In his room, he sat down in the large chair in the corner, took Muffy, and put him on his lap. He wanted to thank his mini-sheep again because he helped so much to save the Kiwi family's egg. "Those were two weird birds, the kiwis, weren't they?" Muffy asked grimly, "they don't even have wings, and they can't fly." "Every animal looks different. They don't all look the way you want them to, Muffy. That's the way it is," Matz replied. Muffy only bleated briefly. Matz had already fallen asleep as he was just too tired. Muffy also made himself comfortable on his lap, fell asleep, and began to snore.

When Matz had fallen asleep, the fairy Hine appeared in his room and began to whisper something into his ear. She whispered to him that he and Muffy had done something wonderful today because they had saved an egg. Maka was also a great help. Any time you can help, that would be good. So Matz was a role model for many. Then she whispered that he would sleep very soundly. If he woke up, he wouldn't remember her. Then the fairy Hine floated away.

It was similar with Maka. She was much too tired to stay awake. When they came home, the father had to carry her upstairs to her room. There he laid her on the bed and wished her a good night, although she didn't hear anything more. She was fast asleep. When she slept like this in her room, the good fairy Hine also appeared there. The fairy whispered in Maka's ear that she was very proud of her and that many more adventures would be waiting for her. Everything would be all right if Maka and her friend Matz were always prepared and showed courage.

Then, Hine said that Maka wouldn't remember anything in the morning and floated away. Maka smiled in her sleep.

There was no school the next day. Maka got up, opened the curtains, and the shining sun greeted her. Outside, there were many sheep bleating in the meadows around their house. She ran down the stairs and skipped into the kitchen.

Her parents had made breakfast for her. She took the tray and went out onto the terrace. There the birds twittered and waved to her. Some shouted, "Hey, Maka. We heard you were helping the Kiwi family. Great! Thank you!" Maka smiled proudly. She ate her breakfast very slowly and enjoyed it. After the wonderful breakfast, she picked up the phone and tried to call Matz.

But Matz didn't hear the phone ringing because he was in the barn. Finally, all of the farm animals had to be fed: the cows, the pigs, and the sheep. Whew! Work was rather hard. The food had to be brought into the stables, and the animals also needed water. Matz was already sweating so early in the morning. It made him happy seeing that the animals were doing well. He was able to help his parents because there is always work on a farm. Mrs. Hen, a chicken, came running excitedly and clucked. "Oh Matz, I heard that you and Maka helped the Kiwi family. I think that's nice. Well, that's good. You did a great job," she cackled in a high voice. "Well, it's terrible that the kiwis always have problems with their eggs. We were happy to help," Matz replied. "Where's the egg now?" the chicken cackled curiously. "It's in the hatchery. We left it to the gamekeepers. They know what they're doing. Now the egg is warm and safe." Then, Matz took an empty bucket of water, waved to Mrs. Hen and walked towards the small pasture behind the house. There, his two ponies waited. He wanted to ride them to see Maka in the morning. Matz and Maka wanted to go to the lake and take a boat ride. They loved the water, and Matz could row and sail very well. In New Zealand, almost everyone can sail well. Whew, I'm sweating a lot, he thought. Perhaps we will soon experience even more adventures or help even more animals.

In the pasture behind the house, he greeted his ponies and put saddles on them. "Where are we going today?" asked one of them. "To Maka's and then a trip to the lake. We want to take advantage of this wonderful day and not just sit around somewhere," said Matz and gently stroked the ponies.

"Okay, darlings, let's go," he shouted as he swung on one of the ponies and rode off. The other pony, he led slightly on a leash next to him.

Suddenly he started to laugh. Stop, he thought, someone is still missing! Right. Muffy! He jumped off the little horse, ran back to the house and up the stairs to his room. Muffy was lying on the chair just as he had fallen asleep yesterday and was snoring. "Hey, hey. Wake up, Muffy," he exclaimed. Then he saw Muffy slowly open one eye and close it again very quickly. Then the mini-sheep opened its mouth wide and yawned. Uh-oh, someone is in a bad mood, Matz thought and said in a soft tone: "I'm going to get a bucket of ice-cold water and pour it on your...". He hadn't finished the sentence when Muffy jumped like lightning from the sofa into his arms. The sheep was so afraid of water. Matz noticed Muffy trembling in his arms and whimpering: "Anything, but water!" He had to laugh. "It's all right. No water for you." Carefully he carried Muffy down the stairs and went outside. He put him on one of the ponies, and they rode away. Muffy was still very sleepy, and grumpily asked: "Where are we going?" "To the lake," came the answer. "No! Please don't." Muffy was terrified and had sheer horror on his face. "Don't worry," Matz said, "You don't have to go in the water. You can wait on the shore." Muffy wasn't happy, but content.

They rode on the same path through the forest as they rode their bikes yesterday. Matz stopped the ponies after a short while and asked Muffy if they had forgotten something. "No," came the answer. "Yes," Matz said, "our helmets!" "Why them?" Muffy asked. "You should also wear a helmet when riding a horse because it's safer," Matz said and took out a helmet. With a mischievous smile, he pulled Muffy's helmet out of his backpack and put it on the sheep. Of course, Muffy thought it made no sense again. Then they rode on. The ponies ambled very slowly, very leisurely. Matz could enjoy nature again today because he could take his time. Yesterday he had to be quick. Now the earth suddenly shook again so that Matz and Muffy lifted from their saddles.

Boom, boom, boom, roared the earth. "Oh, that's pretty bumpy again," Muffy said. Matz thought so too, but it seemed somewhat strange to him again. He had the impression that someone was watching them. He stopped the ponies briefly, and everyone listened.

It was quiet as a mouse; only a light wind blew. Here and there twittered a bird. That's all there was to hear. So he instructed the two ponies to continue trotting slowly. On the way, he also had to calm them down a bit because the two small horses had gotten a bit scared when the earth trembled.

After some time, Matz saw the farm and the house of Maka and her family in the distance. He began to wave as he slowly approached the farm with his ponies. In fact, Maka had noticed them and ran towards them. "I tried to call you," she shouted excitedly and out of breath as she approached. "Hello everyone," she said as Matz jumped off his pony. Then Maka greeted everyone with a hongi.

Only Muffy made a face and was still angry that he had to wear a helmet. Maka stroked the little sheep and said: "You look really cute with your helmet. It suits you." "Well, thanks," Muffy said, "I think I look stupid in a helmet."

Suddenly the magic fairy Hine arrived, who only appeared to the children in their dreams. When she saw the small group, she headed for them all.
"Hello, everyone," called the fairy and flew close to the children. "Maka, Matz, and Muffy, where did you come from? Where are you going?" she asked, "The children were amazed. A fairy! A real fairy. "We want to rest for a moment and then go to the lake. There lies my Waka, my boat," said Matz, who was still completely perplexed.

Then they invited the fairy into the house. She was happy with the invitation. The ponies got water, and everyone else marched into the kitchen, while the fairy flew after them. Muffy wanted to graze in the pasture, so they left the sheep outside.

Sometime later, Maka and Matz sat at the kitchen table. "I wanted to thank you again," said the fairy who was floating above the table in front of them, "you helped the kiwis a lot yesterday." The children sat there with big eyes and stared at the fairy: "How do you know?" The fairy only smiled, "Fairies know things," she said, "What is the matter with the egg?" asked Matz. "We don't know yet, but the gamekeepers are trying very hard to save the little kiwi in the egg," Hine replied. Then she told them that the kiwis in New Zealand were really threatened. No kiwis live in other countries, only in the zoo. Then she briefly flew out of the kitchen and returned with a globe from the next room.

At first, she just turned the globe fast and suddenly stopped it. "Imagine," she said, "this globe is our world, and you live here, in New Zealand." Maka and Matz looked at each other. "Then we'll stand on our heads and fall off some time," Matz said. The fairy Hine smiled. That's the question she expected. "Well, in principle, it is like that, but you don't notice it," she explained, "there is something called gravity. That means it's like a magnet. That's why people don't fall off the earth. When you throw something in the air, it always falls back to Earth." Maka and Matz marveled and listened because the fairy Hine was so kind and could explain it so well. "There's something else," she said, "we're on the southern side of the world. It is sometimes called the Southern Hemisphere. The earth rotates on its own axis. That is why it is sometimes dark and sometimes light, so sometimes day and then night again. Something else interesting is that the earth not only spins like a ball, it also flies in a huge circle around the sun. And what happens?" The two children looked at her with open mouths. They had never heard anything like it in school. That's why they had no answer to the question. Anyway, nobody could explain it as well as Hine the fairy. She held the globe in her left hand and turned the ball slowly. She was flying around the table at the same time. The table should be the sun. "Well, what do you think?" she asked. There was no answer.

"Look at this. Sometimes the Southern Hemisphere is close to the sun, and sometimes the Northern Hemisphere is a little closer. This creates the seasons: spring, summer, fall, and winter." Ah, now it dawned on the children. Maka and Matz watched the fairy turn the globe and slowly fly around the table. "Can the world be stopped?" Matz wanted to know. Hine smiled while flying and replied: "Actually not."

"What would happen if someone stopped the world? Maybe a giant," Maka wanted to know. "Oh, that would be awful," said the fairy, "everything would fly around. All humans and animals would whirl through the air. It's best not to let it go that far. Therefore, you should always look after the earth and always look after other people and animals." The fairy placed the globe in the middle of the table and turned it very slowly. She showed and explained to them all continents: Australia, Asia, Europe, Africa, America, the Arctic in the North and Antarctica in the South. "Maybe we can visit all the continents," Maka said. "Of course," said the fairy, "that's no problem.

You just always have to be well prepared when you want something. Wish, prepare, do, and fight, that must be your motto! Forever." "Yes!" they shouted while raising their arms. Hine was pleased. "Well, my dears," she then said, "I must say goodbye because there are so many children that I want to teach." "Too bad," Maka said somewhat sadly and asked, "Will we see you again?" "I will always be with you," Hine said, "you just have to really believe in me. If you feel lonely and you don't know what to do, or if you think you can't do something, all you have to do is close your eyes and be quiet for a few minutes, and I will help you." Then the fairy Hine waved once more. As a farewell, she said: "Remember that everything in life has meaning, even if you don't see it right away!" So she spoke and slowly floated away.

"That was great," Matz said, "there really is a fairy." "Yes, you just have to believe in them," Maka said. The children sat there for a while and could hardly believe that they had spoken to a fairy. They would have loved to go out into the big world, but they decided that they would go to the lake as planned. They called for Muffy outside the house. The sheep had lazily laid down on the meadow and chewed on long blades of grass. Actually, Muffy didn't want to join them anymore because it was very comfortable on the meadow, and you could easily relax there. Besides, Muffy was panicky about the water again. As the children kept calling for Muffy, the sheep trotted back to them in a bad mood.

Now the two ponies were saddled again, and all were ready to ride to the lake. When Maka and Matz were just a few meters away from the house, Maka barely heard the telephone in the house was ringing. She gave Matz the reins of her pony, jumped off, and sprinted as fast as she could into the house. Some time passed until Matz suddenly heard a cheer outside. So he jumped off the pony and ran towards the house. Then Maka came to meet him and shouted in complete disbelief: "It lives! It's alive! The baby boy of the Kiwi family hatched! One of the gamekeepers just called."

The children were happy and hugged. Then they decided that they should go to the Kiwi family first, instead of riding to the lake.

On the way to the Kiwi family, they did not ride fast because they did not want to exhaust the ponies. During the ride, they talked a lot, laughed often, and imagined what the Kiwi family could do together now. When they arrived at the Kiwis, the two birds stood sadly and alone in front of their small nest as if they had not moved from this spot since the last farewell.

Maka stopped holding the reigns on her pony. She jumped off and ran towards the two birds. "Everything is all right!" she shouted. Then she hugged them and told them about the phone call she had received from the hatchery. Tears were rolling down Mr. and Ms. Kiwi's eyes. They were happy tears. The two hugged with joy, while Maka and Matz stood by and watched

The two children also had tears in their eyes because they were so happy about the Kiwis' happiness. "Hey, now it's time we go back to the hatchery and thank the gamekeepers," Matz shouted. Then the small group set off for the hatchery. This time everyone was happy and chattered as much as they could. They were not as sad this time as their last visit there.

But suddenly, the earth began to tremble again, and everyone was thrown into the air. As they recovered, Maka asked if everyone was all right.

Nobody was seriously injured, only one of the ponies had skin scraped off the leg. Mini-sheep Muffy was lying in a tree and moaned loudest because he wanted all the attention. "Muffy, be quiet!" Matz scolded, "Nothing bad happened to you." Muffy was quiet.

"It's strange," Matz said, "Every time we ride or go somewhere, the earth trembles a bit. I'd like to know why." When everyone got up, the small group set off again to travel the path to the hatchery. After some time, they arrived there, and Mr. and Ms. Kiwi were running around excitedly. One of the gamekeepers greeted them all and led the two birds to the hatchery box with a window. Inside, the little kiwi sat in a nest of grass and was still a little dazed. While Ms. Kiwi waved excitedly at the little one in the glass box, Mr. Kiwi jumped up and down behind her. Maka and Matz took turns, hugging him, and talking to him. Everyone agreed that today was a particularly beautiful day.

After some time, the two kiwis said goodbye and made their way home. The gamekeeper had told them that the boy was healthy, but should stay in the station for a few more days of observation. They could come back any day, he said.

Maka and Matz were visibly relieved. They said goodbye to everyone and rode off waving, after Matz had quickly grabbed Muffy and saddled up his pony. It was a good day. Maka and Matz thought nothing would go wrong, but they were mistaken.

The stupid giant Tikitipua

After some time they reached the lake. There they got off their ponies and let them graze. It was a small lake with water so clear that you could see to the bottom and see all the fish. Nobody had ever dumped waste or oil here and everything was still clean. Around the small lake stood mountains, and there were meadows and forests. Muffy crept away quietly because he was afraid of water. He preferred to be alone and watch Maka and Matz from a distance. Sailing? No thanks that wasn't for a sheep.

Matz, on the other hand, was very much looking forward to his boat, which was floating on the small lake. He was an enthusiastic sailor and could hardly wait to set sail. Maka certainly wanted to accompany him, she too was looking forward to it. But first, she spread out a blanket and made herself comfortable. "Matz," she exclaimed, "If you need help, just call. I'll come and help you." "No, everything's fine," said Matz, who had already tinkered with his boat.

After a while, Matz came back from his boat and beamed because now he was done. Actually, all they had to do was set the sails and they were ready to go. But Maka suggested eating something first. Matz could not say no, and they enjoyed their food. They also enjoyed the wonderful view they had from the meadow.

How beautiful, they both thought and were glad it was really quiet. They could only hear the chirping of the birds, but it seemed to them as if the birds were somewhat worried.

Then suddenly, the calm was over. There it was again, that sound and roar: Boom, boom, boom. The earth trembled again, and the quake came even closer. They were thrown in the air a little, just like their animal friends. It became louder and louder. The earth trembled more and more. Everyone flew higher and higher into the air, even the boat at the jetty overturned. Then suddenly everything was quiet again. Nothing could be heard, except the boat still rocking on the water. Whew, Maka, and Matz looked at each other in surprise. They were sitting in the shade. It was strange because trees were standing pretty far away. They were surprised.

Maka looked up and was shocked. "Ahh, help!" she shouted. With big eyes, she stared up into the face of a giant.

"Help, help, where are you from?" she shouted. Then Matz was frightened too. "Aaaaaah!" he cried, "a giant!" They both looked staring into the face of a young giant, so big that his shadow covered almost the whole country and the lake. They both were amazed. Muffy had also pulled himself together and stared with huge eyes at this great figure. No one had ever seen the sheep like that before. All creatures are quite big for mini-sheep, but this figure was bigger than anything Muffy had ever seen.

"You need not be afraid," said the giant in a deep voice, "I will not harm you, I only want to be your friend." "A beautiful friend that will scare us," Maka shouted, "You're silly, aren't you?" She was still shocked and trembling a little. The giant himself was frightened and also a little sad. That's not what he wanted. He was a sad giant because he had no one to play with and no friends. But Maka and Matz certainly didn't know that. And so they had to recover from shock. There stood the sad giant and he looked down at them. "If you want friends, you have to do something about it. You have to go to the children and ask if you can play or help," Maka said. Matz nodded. "You can't just sneak up on people and scare them if you want them to be your friends. You must help them and you must take care of them," he said, "we have always wondered why the earth trembled so much. So it was you!" Then the sad giant nodded. "Yes," he said, "I've always run after you and haven't dared to speak to you." Now the two of them thoughtfully invited the giant to sit down.

When he fell to the ground next to the two of them, it shook quite a lot again. Boom. That's why everyone near him flew up a little for a moment. But then everyone was relieved. That's when the giant began to tell a story. His name was Tikitipua. He told them that he had no siblings and lived alone with his parents in the mountains. They were always hiding out of fear of being discovered. Since it was so boring for him, he sometimes played tricks on people. Then he stamped his feet so hard that the earth shook a little. The children had experienced this.

Then Maka and Matz realized that the giant Tikitipua wasn't dumb or evil at all. He was just lonely and wanted friends. But sometimes he overdid it when he got boisterous. Then there was no stopping him. "Tikitipua, I must ask you something," Matz said and continued, "you know us now and we know you somewhat. When I look at you, you look strong. Do you have that kind of power?" "Oh, yes," the giant replied with his deep voice, "I have great powers. But sometimes if I'm not careful I destroy something." "So? What can you do with your power?", Maka asked. "I can stop the world," said the giant proudly. "No, you can't," the children laughed, "no one can. You can't stop the world. Everything would fly around like a merry-go-round." "Shall I show you?" asked the giant. "You can try, but even you can't stop the world," Matz blurted. "I'll prove it to you," the giant answered, and he jumped up. The earth trembled a bit again.

Then he made giant steps towards Mount Cook, the highest mountain in New Zealand. Maka and Matz saw from some distance how the giant bent down some and grabbed the top of the big mountain with both hands. Then he pulled at the top of the mountain as if he wanted to move it away. He pressed the heels of his feet firmly into the ground. He grimaced his big round face because he had to put so much effort into it. Maka and Matz watched him with their mouths open. Then it happened. There was a huge jolt, and the earth stood still. It was not peaceful because when the earth stands still, then everything flies around.

And so it was now. It became very loud as if you could hear thousands of trumpets and sirens. Everything was flying around. People tumbled, animals flew by, and a storm came that whirled everything around so that you couldn't see anything. Maka and Matz cried out loud for help.

In their distress, they clung to trees, but the trees did not stay in the ground and their roots were ripped out. Both knew that you had to lie flat on the ground and bend a little to protect themselves, but that didn't help them either. They kept being thrown around. Water, wind, dust, stones, people, animals, everything flew past them. In their misfortune, they were thrown against the foot of another mountain, where they found a little protection. While they were trying to protect each other, they shouted out loud to the giant: "Stop it, stop! Turn the earth again!" Astonished, the giant stood there and watched the world fly in chaos. He still had his hands grasping the top of Mount Cook.

Despite the raging wind and rain that emerged, he heard the children's voices. Because they shouted loudly, he pushed himself with all his might against the top of the mountain and pushed the earth again.

Wind and rain stopped, nothing flew around, and it became quiet. Not a single sound could be heard. Maka and Matz breathed a sigh of relief. They looked at each other with relief and realized that they were not injured. Then they looked at their surroundings. Everything was quiet, but nothing was left in its place. Their eyes fell on the giant and they shouted at him: "Are you crazy? You can't do that! You really stopped the Earth." Tikitipua made a concerned face. "I didn't want that, I didn't want that," he said. Then Matz yelled out: "You should think about what can happen if you do something like that before you do it." He and Maka looked at the giant silently as he stood there with his weepy face and looked back at them.

Then something strange happened. Suddenly the silence was interrupted by a noise in the air. It was a loud hiss as if something was flying through the air at high speed. Maka and Matz looked at something that appeared to be a brown-green ball of wool. This little ball crashed right on the giant's chest. At that moment, he could only shout "Ouch" and fell over as the impact of the little thing was so strong. Everything looked strange somehow. The giant lifted his head a little while lying down, looked at the thing sitting on his chest, and pulled himself together. It was a goblin maki, a little monkey. These animals are also called tarsiers. In some countries they are called makis.

The Maki had flown through the air and crashed into the giant accidentally. The small animal, with its short, greenish fur, its big eyes, and its strange limbs pulled itself together, shook itself off, and looked the giant directly in the eyes with an angry face.

Then the little creature started screaming out loud: "What was that? Who would do that? Why is everything flying around? Did you do that? Where are my friends?" The giant didn't know what happened to him. Who was that little pipsqueak?

Tikitipua slowly rose and took the Maki carefully in his hand. Then he opened his hand and simply held it in front of his chest so that the little creature did not fall down. He went back to Maka and Matz very slowly. He walked very carefully because he was ashamed that he had stopped the world and did not want to make another mistake.

Maka and Matz had also pulled themselves together and shook the dust off their things. Now they watched the giant with amusement as he brought Maki to them. They had never seen such an animal but knew that it was a goblin maki. These animals can climb well and live in small families in Asian jungles. It is often very hot there. Makis are nocturnal, so they usually go looking for food at night. They catch worms, insects, beetles, and spiders with their long fingers. The small animals have huge eyes so that they can see well at night. And because they have such big eyes, they actually look very odd, but also very cute. Makis can only live in Asia because it is not only very warm, but also very humid.

The animals need this climate. Therefore, Maka and Matz knew immediately that the Maki could not live here in New Zealand. Now the animal sat on the hand of the giant Tikitipua and scolded and yelled at him. Tikitipua was slowly approaching. As he stood in front of the two children, he slowly put Maki down and made a sad face again.

"Now look at this chaos," the Maki shouted with his high, squeaky voice, "I'm so cold." Matz rummaged through his backpack, which he carried with him and pulled out a scarf. He wrapped this around the Maki to protect him. Then the children wanted to put him in Muffy's fur to keep the little animal warm. But where was Muffy? Where were their ponies? At first, they heard a miserable bleating and looked up.

There Muffy was hanging in the branch of a big tree. "Help him get down," Maka asked the giant. He carefully took the mini-sheep from the tree. Then they heard a neighing from a long way away. On the back of the hillside, the two ponies hung from a cliff.

Tikitipua went to them very carefully, without stomping hard, took them off the cliff and put the horses on the ground. They were really shook up. Meanwhile, Maka and Matz looked around the area. There was rubble everywhere and many trees had fallen. Overall, it didn't look good.

So they decided to clean up as much as they could. The giant helped them and they could save some animals. At the lake, Tikitipua lifted a fallen tree with two fingers. Underneath was a family of ducks, who marched to the lake and swam away. He also took trees from the cliffs that were thrown up there and put animals on the ground again. It was quite exhausting, but everyone helped as best they could. The giant still had a guilty conscience and worked hard to clean up.

When they took a break, Maka discovered that the Maki was shaking. "I am coooold," he squeaked. "Oh boy," Maka said, "it seems we have to do something." "Like what?" Matz asked. "Say, you little goblin maki," he said, looking at the little greenish goblin, "where exactly do you live?" "In Borneo," Maki replied in a shaking voice, "I want to go home." The giant stood next to them with an anxious face and Muffy looked at them questioningly. Only the ponies stood somewhat far away and ate. "Well, let's go to Borneo!" Matz shouted and stretched his fist up high. "Yes, we must do that," Maka said and sighed a little. They could no longer sail because it was more important to bring the Maki back.

Well, a plan was needed. How could they prepare such a long trip on short notice? Matz pulled out a map. He always had everything in his backpack that you need to survive: water, a vitamin bar, compass, knife, flashlight, ropes, cords.

First, they had to cross to the coast of New Zealand and then to Australia. From there, they would march to northern Australia and then sail to Asia. Matz, after all, was an expert in sailing, like so many here in the country. Then everyone got ready for the ride to the coast and off they went. Only Tikitipua wanted to stay and clean up. But he promised to come as soon as possible.

On the way to Australia

Maka and Matz rode very slowly, to not overexert the two ponies. They knew this ride to the coast would take a long time. Matz held Muffy in front of him firmly with both hands. The Maki was stuck in his thick fur so he wouldn't get cold. He was wrapped up like an Eskimo, only his big eyes looked out of the clothes the children had dressed him in. And so the two ponies trotted very slowly, step by step, all day long. As they had to ride west, Matz repeatedly pulled out his compass and checked whether they had taken the right direction. Slowly it was getting dark Maka and Matz agreed to set up camp and stay overnight. The ponies stood in the grass and ate, while Maka and Matz collected sticks and large leaves.

They wanted to build a small lodging for the night. Matz stuck the sticks into the ground and built a scaffold. Maka placed the leaves and the wood they had found on the scaffolding so that it looked like a small house. It had a roof, four walls, and a small entrance. Even if it rained, they would be protected. And soon it was really dark.

So everyone squeezed their way through the small entrance and snuggled up together because it was getting really cold at night. Precisely that was not good for Maki because a maki always needs warmth. They still had to convince him that he would soon be home. Perseverance and struggle was now the motto. They had to make it and they wanted to bring Maki home. His home, where it was really warm. It wasn't long before they all fell asleep. Matz woke up at night because Muffy snored so loud. But Muffy was so tired that he slept soundly.

As they lay and slept, the fairy Hine came again. Hine spoke to them and thanked them for doing so much to bring Maki home. It was a real adventure and it would be worth it, she said, because they did something good. The fairy wished them a good night and promised that everything would be all right. Then she floated silently away.

The next morning everyone woke and got ready and continued riding. It wasn't much further to the coast, a few more hours at most. And as they rode, Maka asked: "Hey Maki, we've known you for a few hours now. What are we supposed to call you?" "Maki," came the grumpy answer from Muffy's fur. Maki was snuggled in there so that only his big eyes could be seen, but it was not really warm for the small, greenish animal. That's why there were always only short, cheeky answers. "Ha, ha," laughed Matz, "then we'll just call you Maki. Fine." On the way to the coast, they took a break from time to time.

Everywhere they stopped to rest, strangers helped them. They always got something to eat, to drink, or could wash themselves. It was so good when they could eat fresh fruit that the farmers gave them, or when they were offered water or tea. The animals were always supplied. The ponies got water and food; even Muffy slurped with full enthusiasm what was offered to him. But unfortunately, the mini-sheep often had to be warned because he constantly burped after the meal and never thanked the farmers. Maki imitated Muffy and belched as well. So the two cheeky animals often had a burping contest. Maka and Matz had to speak harsh words and make it clear to them that this was very rude. Maka and Matz were always so happy about the help of strangers that they decided to help other people, too, if they needed help. But now they had another mission because they had to reach the coast and sail to Australia.

After a few hours, the time had come, and they were standing on the coast: "Yes, hooray," the children shouted, "We made it!" The ponies were neighing,

Muffy bleated, and Maki shrieked with pleasure. But their joy did not last long. When they looked around, they saw many boats ashore. Most of them were destroyed. The holes in the bottom of the boats were quite big, and the sails were torn. So it would take a long time to get them fixed. That was severe because, in New Zealand, almost everyone can sail, and a New Zealander without a sailboat is like an airplane without wings. The people around them also had no time to help them because they were all busy and had to clean up. What could you do? Matz had an idea.

"We'll build a raft and sail it to Australia," he declared. But Maka warned that it would take too long for a whole raft to be ready. So they were still at a loss. They talked to each other and made suggestions. But none of the suggestions were good enough. Nevertheless, they had to go to Australia to get to Maki's home in Borneo, Asia. Slowly Maka and Matz became a little sad. Muffy also seemed a little grumpy and annoyed.

Maki became more and more concerned because although the little animal was stuck in Muffy's fur, he slowly became cold. The friends became sadder and sadder because there was no solution in sight. Maka said that there must always be a way out or a solution. She learned that from the fairy Hine. "Well, folks, cheer up! We have to do something," she said. All of a sudden, everyone was talking again, making suggestions and fluttering their arms. Even the two ponies discussed ideas with them. Suddenly the earth boomed again, and it was the typical boom, boom, boom sound that they all knew. And again, everyone flew up a bit, the earth trembled so strongly. But this time, they were happy because they knew that the giant Tikitipua was coming. Then he stood in front of them and was a little out of breath.

"Hello, there you are," he said in his deep voice and asked, "What is it?" "We stand here because all the boats have been destroyed, so we don't know how to get to Australia," Maka said. "Can't you swim to Australia?" Tikitipua asked. "Well, you're a very clever giant, my dear," Matz said. "Of course, we can swim, but it is more than 2,000 kilometers, which is more than 1,200 miles, to the coast of Australia. Do you know how far that is?" he asked the giant. "Ohhhh, that's far," he said. Matz then asked him: "Do you know how deep the water in the ocean between New Zealand and Australia is?" "No one's ever swum over there," Maka said, "that's too deep for you, too." Tikitipua stood there with his arms hanging and stared at the ocean. "Yes, it's deep," he said, "but I can swim there and carry you. Every child should learn to swim."

Maka and Matz looked at each other in wonder. "I just need to hurry home and get my hat," boomed Tikitipua, "I'll be right back." Again Maka and Matz stared at each other without understanding while the giant stomped away and caused the earth to tremble. They didn't know what he was talking about. They continued to sit along the coast with the animals and thought about how best to get to Australia.

After a while, Tikitipua came back. You could hear it again: boom, boom, boom. Then he stood before them and rejoiced. His giant face was as big as the moon, and when he laughed, it looked as if the moon in the sky was laughing. Tikitipua held something in his hand that looked like a huge blue cake, and it was the size of a football stadium.

But it wasn't a cake; instead, it was a hat. Maka, Matz, the ponies, Muffy and Maki, stared up into the giant's big moon face. They all had their mouths wide open and they were so amazed: "Yes, you can be astonished," the giant grumbled with his deep voice, "This is my aunt's hat. There's room for all of you in it. Then I'll put it on and swim over to Australia with you all in it. Without a boat." Everyone looked at each other in wonder. "Can you swim at all?" Maki yelled. "Of course," Tikitipua replied, "I can swim very well. Everyone can swim, you just have to practice." "But you are a giant! You're bigger than a whale," Maki continued saying. "You'll see," Tikitipua replied, "I'll do my best because I don't want to make another big mistake and put others in danger." Now a decision had to be made. Should they all really get on the giant's hat and let him take them to Australia? Maka called for a vote. "Well, everybody, listen up," she said, "We have to decide if we want to do this. Those in favor, raise your hand. The majority decides." Maka and Matz raised their hands. The two ponies were also adventurous and lifted their hooves.

Only Muffy and Maki seemed afraid. Muffy was afraid of water, and Maki didn't want to either. "Well, the decision is clear, and most are in favor," said Maka, "it's about taking Maki first to Australia and then by boat to Asia. Now we have no boat, and Tikitipua is our only hope." Muffy and Maki trembled all over because they feared swimming in the ocean." All right, if you say so," Maki said, "I just want to go home. Then it must be."

"Good," Matz said, "of course it won't be a real pleasure, but when can you swim across the ocean in a huge hat?" Then he turned to Tikitipua, who promised to be very careful. “Promise, scout’s honor,” he said. "Here we go, folks," Matz shouted, "let's get ready for the trip." First, we discussed what we would need for this journey because they would complete a sea voyage of about 2,000 kilometers. It would be a long journey, and storms could occur: Life jackets, food, drink, and animal food. So everyone headed out and helped. Life jackets were lying around on the beach because many places had not yet been cleaned up. The animals collected enough food for themselves. Maka and Matz also found an old, intact rowing boat that was lying on the beach. This could be used wonderfully as a spare boat, if anyone fell into the water or if the giant got tired.

Then the giant lifted them all very slowly and carefully onto his hat. On the top of the hat, they all felt quite lost as the area was large. At least they could stand on the edge and look out to sea.

The moment arrived when the giant slowly raised his hat and would put it on. "Just be careful," Maki shrieked. The giant was so frightened that his hand trembled some, and so the whole big hat did too. They had to hold on tight so as not to be thrown around again. "All right, now very carefully into the water, Tikitipua," Matz called from above, and the giant moved very slowly towards the sea. Although everyone had a great view from the hat, they were still not comfortable.

Slowly the giant entered into the water. When the water splashed to his chin, they were already very far from the coast. Tikitipua glided very carefully through the water. He did not move his head so that his hat always sat straight on his head, and nothing could happen to the children and animals. Then he was in the water with his whole body and began to swim slowly. When the children realized that he was really moving very carefully, they became more relaxed. Now they could all enjoy the wonderful view from above.

Behind them, New Zealand disappeared in the fog, otherwise only the ocean could be seen. It was kind of exciting. Only for Muffy and Maki, it was totally boring. They could not look beyond the edge of the hat. Besides, they were afraid of all that water. So, many hours passed on the ocean between New Zealand and Australia.

After a while, Matz was suddenly electrified. He saw a big worm swimming in the water. No, that couldn't be a worm. "Maka," he shouted, "look!" Maka also couldn’t believe her eyes. There was a whale swimming down there, and it was faster than the giant. The whale enjoyed swimming with the giant. Sometimes he would dive down, and you could see his big tailfin. Then he suddenly shot out of the water entirely and dropped. The water splashed almost up to the hat. It was a fantastic spectacle. Maka and Matz had often observed whales. They often came into the waters around New Zealand, but they have never been so close to one of these huge mammals.

Although whales look like big fish and live only in the water, they are not fish. They are mammals because the young are nursed by their mother. But what was that? There was something about that whale. Indeed. The animal was caught in a large net that fishermen had left somewhere in the ocean. Unfortunately, the whale got into the net and was caught.

"Hey, Tikitipua!" Maka and Matz shouted to the giant, "see the whale?" "Yes!" sounded the deep voice of the giant who had concentrated on swimming. "Can you help him and free him from the net?" But now it's getting shaky, the giant thought, and tried to keep balance in the water, so everyone in the hat was not shaken. Then he grabbed the whale with one hand while swimming. When he had grabbed it, he straightened up a little and just paddled with his legs underwater. With his free hand, Tikitipua plucked the net from the whale and freed him. Up in the hat, the children cheered and the whale shot out of the water again with joy. For days he had swum with the net around his body through the ocean and was already exhausted. Now he was rid of it and got his freedom back. Then the whale turned away. Maka and Matz waved.

They had the impression that the grateful whale was waving back when he threw himself on his side one last time and then swam away. "That was so beautiful," Maka said, "but unfortunately, there are still many people who let the oceans get filthy and throw garbage into them." Then they shouted down: "Tikitipua, that was great! You did a good job." The giant was happy that he could help and swam slowly, very happily on.

However, Maka, Matz and the animals in the hat became quite bored over time. Just looking at the sea was pretty dull. What should we do to fight boredom? Well, first, everyone sat in a circle and deliberated once again. First, Matz checked with the compass and a sea chart to see whether the giant was still swimming in the right direction. Then Maka asked everyone to tell their funniest experience. Each person took a turn. Everyone mostly laughed at what was told.

Then Maki began to tell a little more about himself. Although it got a little warmer at sea, Maki shivered and snuggled into Muffy's fur. In his story, the children learned a lot about his homeland, the jungle and his family. They lived in small trees, on branches and in big bushes. At night they climbed down to find insects. Makis can see particularly well at night because they have big eyes. Maki said that some people would catch them and keep them as pets. The little makis belong in the rainforest and need their freedom.

The children learned that it is increasingly difficult to live in the rainforest. More and more trees are simply being cut down because somewhere in the world someone wanted a table made of rainforest wood. "Why does a table have to be made of such wood," Maki asked angrily, "we need our trees because we live there." Furthermore, everyone learned that people there simply cut down trees to make room for plantations. If this continued, there would soon be nothing left of the rainforest. Maki raised his long, rubbery index finger and spoke like a professor: "I warn everyone! The rainforest is also called the 'green lung' because it produces a lot of good air. When the rainforest dies, so do all the animals that live in it. Besides, it'll leave us all breathless."

"You're right," Maka said and shook her head sadly. Suddenly one of the ponies neighed, it had risen and looked over the edge of the hat. "Land in sight!" it whinnied.

Everyone jumped up and ran to the edge. Only Muffy took his time and ran very slowly to the others. After all, the sheep was much too small and could not see over the edge anyway.

"Australia!" everyone shouted and danced with joy. "Yes, that's Australia up ahead. It's about time. I'm pretty tired and exhausted from swimming," said the giant with his deep voice. Now everyone was excited again and ran back and forth. They also noticed how the sun was burning. Matz called to the giant: "Keep swimming carefully until you feel firm ground under your feet. Then, straighten up very slowly." "All right, I'll remember that," came the answer.

The long march through Australia

After many hours at sea, they went ashore in Australia. Tikitipua straightened up very slowly so that the hat did not shake or tilt in only one direction. He was a bit exhausted himself because he had to swim for a long time. On the beach, the water ran down him like little waterfalls, so his shirt and shorts were soaked. Very slowly, he knelt down and carefully took his hat off his head. The friends couldn't wait to get ashore.

Tikitipua took care that everyone came to the beach safe and unharmed, and of course, everyone was happy. Only now did they realize how warm it was and how merciless the sun was. Only Maki had no problems with the heat. He liked it, for him it should always be this nice and warm. But Maki didn't like the beautiful sandy beach because sand was not what a Maki needs. Maka, Matz and the ponies were happy and went for a swim. Yes, it had to be, here on the east coast of Australia. Muffy and Maki stood on the beach and watched them. Muffy was happy standing in the shadow of the giant as he had laid down to rest.

After a short time, Maka, Matz and the ponies were refreshed. Actually, they started going to the north of the country. But suddenly Matz became sad and said: "I think it is much too hot for a sheep. We probably have to walk far on the continent and later through rainforests and deserts. The climate is not good for Muffy." Then he turned to the sheep and said: "Muffy, it's probably best if Tikitipua takes you back." Everyone had sad faces. Of course, Muffy wanted to stay with his friends, but the sheep didn't really feel up to a long walk. Although it was difficult, it was time to say goodbye. Everyone had to realize that they were on the verge of a long march. Such a long march through harsh land would be torture for a mini sheep, like Muffy. Matz was right. It was best for Muffy to return home.

Everyone hugged the small, woolly sheep once more to say goodbye. Then Tikitipua put Muffy back on his hat. Everyone waved goodbye and shouted: "Bye, Muffy. We'll see you soon!" The giant took the hat up very slowly and sat it on his head. Then he walked slowly back into the water and swam slowly away.

Maka, Matz, Maki and the horses watched the giant until he disappeared on the horizon. They were all sad. Maka held Maki in her arms and looked at the sea. She had tears in her eyes, but she knew that it was the best thing for the sheep. Besides, they'll surely see Muffy again soon.

After they got used to the idea that Muffy was gone, Matz pulled out his compass and a map. Then he decided that they should not only walk on the beach but first go to the center of Australia and then north. Then he asked Maka if she agreed with his plan. However, he also knew that it would be tough for the two ponies because they had a long way to walk through an unknown territory, with heat and potential danger. Maka nodded in agreement. "Let's go," Matz said enthusiastically. So they began their ride west to the interior of Australia.

After a long time, the landscape changed, and they rode through forests and brush. Matz took a closer look at the trees and said: "Hm. Look at these trees, Maka. Such trees don't grow at home." "Right," Maka replied, "these are eucalyptus trees. They grow almost exclusively here."

"Look there, look there, look up there," Maki suddenly screamed and pointed towards a treetop, "There sits a teddy bear eating leaves!" Maka, who now had Maki on her pony, had to laugh. Matz also thought it was funny. "No, no, Maki, they're not teddy bears, even if they sometimes look like that. They're koalas. They only eat eucalyptus," Maka said, waving to one of the koala bears. The small, grey, fuzzy koala bear waved back and climbed very slowly from the eucalyptus tree. He wanted to welcome the unusual visitors.

"You look funny," Maki shouted. Maka scolded: "Maki, you can't insult other animals or people just because they look different!" "You're right," Maki said, "but they look so funny." Then the children took a break to talk with the koala. The koala slowly came down from the tree and smiled. Maki was particularly curious and started immediately with questions: "Tell me, why are you called koalas? The little bear just laughed and said: "Koala means 'the one who does not drink.' Other animals must always drink. We only eat eucalyptus leaves. They contain so much water that we don't always have to drink." Oh my, that impressed Maki.

Then Maka and Matz wanted to know even more about the koalas. And so the little bear began to talk about himself and his friends. The children learned that there are not so many koalas anymore in Australia. Animals are protected there, but not the forests that they live in. Here the people cut down more eucalyptus trees. If there is no more eucalyptus, then we have nothing to eat," said the koala, "dingoes and wild dogs roaming the forests are also dangerous for us." Maka and Matz couldn't believe it. So there were animals again that weren't doing well. The Koalas had similar problems, just like the Kiwis at home in New Zealand. How long would it be before they didn't exist? As a farewell, they embraced the small, fuzzy koala bear and bid him farewell with a typical hongi from their homeland, the greeting by rubbing their noses together. So the koala bear had learned something again and was happy. Then they rode through the forests of Australia, while the koala watched them for a long time.

When it got late, they stopped at a clearing that had water and decided to spend the night. This was necessary because the ponies needed water urgently. Maka and Matz were also tired and hungry. Only Maki felt well, he crossed his legs, stretched out on a bush, and watched the area. The group had stopped directly at a small stream, where clean, clear water flowed. The ponies bent over to drink, while Matz was already gathering wood for a small fire.

Suddenly something rushed in the undergrowth, but nobody saw anything. All of a sudden, Maka was shocked and cried out loudly. In front of her lay a large brown snake on the floor, which looked very dangerous. Then the snake went over to attack. But this was the signal for Maki. From his bush, Maki had observed the whole scene, and without hesitation, he acted just like at home in his native jungle. Maki jumped between Maka and the snake, raised his small rubbery arms, and screamed loudly at the dangerous snake. The snake was so horrified that it immediately moved to the side and got away. Maka was still standing there petrified. "Thank you, Maki," she stammered. "No problem," came the answer.

Matz had also observed the scene and came closer. "Maki, you did a great job, but it was also dangerous," he said. Maki replied: "This is what we do at home when poisonous snakes want to attack our families. Sometimes it helps to scream out loud. Not always, but sometimes." Maki felt like a hero, a hero who had saved someone, and strolled calmly back to his bush. Matz took Maka in his arms and asked if everything was all right. She said yes. Then Matz began to explain: "Snakes don't really want to attack people. You just have to allow them to retreat. All you had was bad luck, Maka, that you were in the way, and the snake could not escape. But everything's all right now."

A little later, everyone sat around the small campfire that Matz had lit and talked about their experiences during the day. Because it had been an exhausting day, they all fell asleep very quickly. As so often, the fairy Hine appeared and whispered in Maka's and Matz's ears. She said that Maka and Matz had once again achieved a lot and acted in an exemplary manner. There is still a long and difficult road ahead of them, but they will get there. Then she floated away.

The next morning they were all pretty tired from the events of the last days. Maka and Matz had to admit that they had imagined the trip a little easier.

Traveling can teach you a lot, but it can also be quite strenuous. So they took it slow at first and ate breakfast. Then Matz pulled out his map and compass and familiarized himself with the route they wanted to take today. Maka took care of the ponies during this time. As they were about to leave, Matz jokingly shouted: "Mount!" Maka smiled, swung on her pony and called for Maki. She remembered that she hadn't seen Maki for a few minutes.

Where was that little round pipsqueak? "Hey, Maki, we want to take off," she shouted. Matz also shouted: "Where are you? Come out of the bushes, we want to go!" But nothing moved. At first, they thought Maki was playing a joke with them. Then, they became restless. Where was Maki? Their hearts beat faster. What if Maki got lost or was in danger? None of them knew the Australian jungle. So they started their search. To be on the safe side, they left the ponies behind and set out on foot in the surrounding area.

At first, they moved only around the place where they had stayed overnight. Then they expanded their search a little, but there was no trace of Maki, however much they searched and shouted. They were desperate. Maka and Matz had to sit down, they were so exhausted. What should they do now? They had taken the long journey and all their hardships, only to bring the little green pipsqueak with his big eyes to his homeland. Now they were sitting without him in a foreign country. Oh, yes, it was exasperating.

Suddenly the branches of the bushes near them bent apart, and in front of them stood a slender, tan girl with dark black hair. She had a long white stripe over her face that almost reached from one ear to the other. On her forehead were other ornaments, small squares, and circles painted in all colors. She had also painted white stripes on her arms and legs. At first, they caught their breath. Who was that? Who was this creature in the middle of the jungle? But then her eyes fell on the little green pipsqueak with the big eyes, which she held in her hand and smiled.

"Maki!" both called at the same time and jumped up. Maki took things quite calmly. He had made himself comfortable in the girl's hand as if he were sitting in a taxi cab. Maka carefully took Maki out of the hands of the stranger and stroked the little ball of wool. "We've been looking for you. We were so afraid for you," she said, "Don't panic, Arika has everything under control," Maki said, "Fine," Matz said, "but you gave us quite the scare. Now you're acting as if nothing had happened. That's not fair!" Maki looked concerned.

The strange girl said in a low voice: "Hello, my name is Arika and I found your friend. The animal was lost." Then Maka and Matz introduced themselves to the girl, and they all went back to the ponies. There Maka and Matz shared the remaining food with Arika and Maki. After all, they had become very thirsty. Since their new friend seemed very extraordinary, they had many questions.

So they learned that Arika belonged to the Australian Aborigines, the natives of Australia. She and her tribe used to live off what nature gave them. That's why they knew how to survive in the rainforest or desert. And how to find food and water. Today most of them lived in towns and villages, just like other Australians. "My name Arika means 'water lily,'" she said.

Of course, Maka and Matz also wanted to know what the paintings on her forehead, face, and arms meant. "These are traditional patterns. Just like in other countries, our men and women wear these traditional body paints. However, these paintings have a deeper meaning for us. They are one of our traditions," explained Arika. Maka and Matz were thrilled. Then Arika made them an offer: "If you want, you can visit with me and stay with my family for a while. Later, someone can certainly lead you north to your destination. Our men are good trackers."

They didn't have to think long about that. Quickly the things were packed and loaded on the ponies again. "This time, you stay very close to us and don't sneak away again," Maka warned and looked at Maki punishingly. Maki just looked at her with his huge eyes and nodded a little cranky. Then they continued on again.

With the Aborigines

The small group was now led by Arika. She knew the way and knew the dangers lurking in the jungle. They went through an incredibly warm, dense jungle with green plants and trees, unknown animals and unfamiliar noises. Maka and Matz were sweating, so it was important for them to drink a lot. Only Maki felt very comfortable in this climate. Since Arika knew the way, they made rapid progress. On the way, Maka and Matz had a lot of questions. They wanted to know everything about the plants and animals in Australia. Arika answered willingly.

As they made their way through the rainforest, they heard a strange sound in the distance. It was a long deep tone as if someone with a deep voice was moaning all the time. "What is that?" Maka asked. "You'll see," Arika said with a smile, "we'll be right there." The children were happy because the march through the Australian jungle was quite exhausting.

The sound became louder and louder. Soon they reached a clearing, and Maka and Matz saw a man sitting, who was blowing into a long pipe, making the sound they had heard for many kilometers. He was slim and also wore the traditional painting on his body and face.

Maka and Matz had never seen such a musical instrument and asked Arika about it. "This is a didgeridoo," she explained, "a hollow, long tree trunk into which you blow. Then, it makes the sounds that you hear. It looks very simple, but you have to practice a long time to make the right notes." Maka and Matz were amazed and enthusiastic. Matz wanted to know if he could play too. But first, Arika introduced them to the man. "This is Apari," she said, pointing at him, "he's one of our best trackers. Apari did not let himself be stopped and continued blowing into his didgeridoo. He just winked at them with his eyes.

Then Arika introduced her new friends to her whole family and then to all the other members of the village community. Maka and Matz were thrilled, only Maki grumbled and wanted something to eat.

Maka and Matz immediately realized that the Aborigines lived in harmony with nature in the small village. They also had the impression that everyone here was very happy, despite the hard life.

Arika's mother invited everyone to dinner. They could not say no, after all, the journey through the jungle had been arduous, and they were now tired and hungry. After dinner, the whole tribe came together and was curious about who Arika had brought with her. Maka and Matz told stories about their adventures, their hike in New Zealand, their journey across the sea to Australia and their way through the Australian rainforest. They also said they were a little scared when they walked through the jungle.

Everyone sitting there in a large circle around them had to laugh. They knew their country and knew exactly how to behave.

Then Maka introduced Maki to everyone as the little animal crawled out of her jacket pocket. Maki was too tired and had slept in her jacket pocket. Now he looked so surprised and tired that everyone had to laugh again. The Aborigines had never seen a Maki, and they all wanted to pet it. Maki kept quiet and endured everything out of hospitality. A little later, Arika's mother showed them where to sleep, and it didn't take long for Maka and Matz to fall asleep to the sounds of the didgeridoo.

When they woke up the next morning, all the villagers were already preparing food. Arika wished them a good morning: "Well, you two are late risers. You guys were tired, huh?" Still quite sleepy, Matz replied: "You can say that out loud. I would like to stay a little longer, but we want to bring Maki home as soon as possible. That's why we have to keep moving." "Too bad," Arika said, "I thought you could stay a little longer." Maki had listened to everything and peered out from under a blanket. "But I want to go home," was his comment. "Don't worry," Maka interrupted, "we're moving on today so you can finally go back to your homeland." "Wonderful," Maki mumbled and crawled back under the blanket. Then they had breakfast. The plan for the trip North was determined. Arika suggested that Apari could show them the way. Maka and Matz agreed.

Apari was a quiet man who knew everything about Australia's nature and knew the way. He also spoke with a friendly voice and calm words. But he warned the two children that it would be a difficult journey. "We must first cross a desert, then another jungle," he said. He also said that they could see a lot of beautiful nature and observe many animals. Then Maka, Matz and Arika became sad as it was time to say goodbye.

They hugged each other and Maka and Matz said goodbye with their traditional hongi. Then Arika stroked Maki again and wished him a good journey. "I know how hard it is for you," she said, "I also want to live here with nature. This is my home, and of course, you want to go back to yours." Maki looked at her with his big eyes. Arika had the impression that Maki was a bit sad. Then they took off.

With Apari through the desert

Maka, Matz, Maki, and the horses were now led by Apari. He knew every path, every animal and every plant here in his homeland. Like all Aborigines, he knew where to find waterholes, which was important to survive in a harsh environment. It was very warm, and yet they had to move on. Maki would finally be brought home. Because they first had to reach the coast in the North, they hiked through the wilderness. Apari always went first. He explored the waterholes because in this heat everyone had to drink a lot and often. The sun was so hot that they had to wear hats and long-sleeved clothing to protect themselves. If they didn't, Apari warned that they could get sunburned.

"Whew," Maka said, "I'm all sweaty again. And it's only morning." Matz agreed with her: "Yes, it is hot and arduous here, but we have to go through it. We've got to make it." Maki leaned back in Maka's lap and said: "Well, then let's do it. I feel warmer than ever. I couldn't take a step in the sand here. I must rest in this heat." Everyone laughed at the little ball of wool as they called it, up there on Maka's pony. You could see it in the faces of the children that it was getting harder and harder for them to move in this heat.

To motivate them, Apari told them that he would soon show them all something unusual and unique. They were all excited, of course. But it became more and more difficult for them to move through the grassland in this heat. More and more often, they had to take a break. As a result, they progressed only slowly. They also had to think about the horses because they needed breaks. And so the small group moved only with difficulty through the steppe of the hot sand, in which the sun burned mercilessly.

In the evening, they rested and built themselves a small shelter of branches and leaves. Apari managed to start a fire, and now they were sitting around in a circle listening to Apari's stories. He spoke of his ancestors who lived in Australia many thousands of years ago and whose habits only changed after settlers came to the continent.

Because it was a tough day, they all fell asleep quickly. That night the fairy Hine reappeared for Maka and Matz. She praised them and told them that they had ridden bravely and that it was all right to rest now. She also said that the next day they would see big animals and could marvel at a natural wonder. Then Hine floated away again.

The next morning Apari said, "Hello, wake up," and he gently woke up the two children. Maka and Matz would have loved to sleep more, but there was still a long way to go. After a short breakfast, all things were packed up, and off they went. As always, it was very hot in the morning. As they walked and rode, the children realized that they were now in an area where there were many more bushes and shrubs.

"Look, a giant rabbit," Maka suddenly shouted. Indeed, there lay an animal, in the shade of the bushes, with reddish fur that looked somewhat like a big rabbit. The animal had laid down on its side and chewed on a blade of grass. Apari went ahead and talked to the animal, then he waved to the children. "Don't worry," he shouted, "come here, I want you to meet someone." Slowly and a little anxiously, the children approached. Maki also had anxious big eyes. As they approached, they noticed that there was not a rabbit in the shade, but a kangaroo.

"That's Boomer," Apari said, pointing to the kangaroo in the shade. "Oh, hello," Maka and Matz replied. The kangaroo lay on its side and lifted its left front leg as a greeting. "He's a little tired," Apari explained, "Kangaroos don't like the heat of the day. Just like you," he added with a smile. "True," said the kangaroo in the shade, "we'd rather just lay about in this heat." Only now did the children realize how big the kangaroo really was. Apari noticed their astonishment and explained:

"Boomer and his wife Kyle are among the tallest existing kangaroos. Because their fur is a bit reddish, they are also called Red Giants. "They grow as big as humans and can jump very well."

Maka, Matz, and Maki were amazed. They had never heard of such big kangaroos. "Where's your wife?" Maki wanted to know. "She's not far away. She needs extra rest because she's got a young joey in her pouch again," came the answer. The children wanted to see the joey. "Don't disturb her," Apari said, "she needs her rest." Apari then explained to them that the young in a kangaroo pouch were only as tiny as a worm at birth. Then he added: "Kangaroo mothers always have a young joey in their pouch. This ensures the survival of their species. Sometimes there are long periods of drought, no water, nothing to eat for the animals, and many of them would perish. But it's not so bad right now." The children were reassured.

Then they heard Apari ask the giant kangaroo a question. Boomer, the lazy kangaroo in the shade, pointed only in one direction and said something like Ullu Ullu. They waved goodbye to him and marched on. "What is Ullu Ullu?" Matz asked. Apari had to laugh. "You misunderstood something. You must be talking about Uluru. That's what the kangaroo said. You will soon see who or what Uluru is," he said and made an excited face. So they moved on to the North. Maki thought upon saying goodbye: "Kangaroos are cool. I want to doze in the shade all day, too."

In the late afternoon, they were sweating and tired again. But in the distance, they suddenly saw a big red lump. "Look in front of us," Apari shouted, pointing at the lump, "that's Uluru." Maka and Matz didn't really know what he meant. But as they got closer and closer to the red lump, they marveled more and more. In front of them lay a huge mountain, a rock that shone bright red in the evening sun. In the middle of Australia. In the middle of the desert. It was fantastic!

Then Maka and Matz saw Apari standing in front of the mountain in awe. "This is Uluru," he said, "Uluru is a special mountain for us. It appears in many of our stories and has a lot to do with our dreams. Other Australians call it Ayers Rock. Every year thousands of tourists come here to take pictures. It is also one of Australia's landmarks. But for us, the mountain is more than that. To us, it is sacred."

They decided to spend the night near the holy mountain. At the evening campfire, Apari told stories and legends of his ancestors, the Aborigines. The children listened eagerly, and they hung on his every word. Nobody dared to interrupt him. Even Maki thought the stories were quite interesting. But after the hardships of the last day, it soon became time for everyone to rest again. This time they spent the night in the open air. It was a unique experience for Maka and Matz to look into the stars before falling asleep.

The next day they left Ayers Rock, which the Aborigines call Uluru, behind and headed north. Their destination was the city of Darwin. It was still a long way, but from there, they could sail by boat to Borneo and bring Maki home. Again it was incredibly hot, but luckily they could spend most of the time on the back of the horses. For Maki, it was always boring. Maki usually rode with Maka in front, on the horse, but had not much else to do. However, Maki was talking all the time.

On the way north, they saw some houses from time to time. Sometimes they even passed small settlements. The friendly farmers waved to them or gave them food and drinks and also supplied the horses with water. They even saw a herd of sheep. "We could have taken Muffy, our mini sheep," Matz said. Apari said: "It's better that your mini sheep is at home. You have to get used to this climate. I'm sure your Muffy would've had trouble with the heat." "You're right," Matz replied and sighed. Maka said: "We can write Muffy and Tikitipua a postcard before we sail across the sea again and bring Maki home." "I've never written a postcard," Apari said, "but before you can write one, we have to cross the desert and through a jungle. "There's still a long way to Darwin City." The children nodded, the ponies swayed, and Maki just shrugged his shoulder.

And so they moved on. It was just as Apari had predicted, it was really hard, but everyone tried. With all their strength, they rode through the Australian desert to the north for days. Every evening the children and the animals fell asleep exhausted. But Apari knew the way, knew where to find water points and led the group safely.

After many days of riding through the desert, nature slowly changed. They saw more and more palm trees and other plants. The air became hot and humid. Because there were so many rivers, small lakes and swamps, other animals such as turtles, crocodiles, snakes and birds lived here. As they rode through the jungle, Maka looked up and suddenly shouted:

"Oh, look at the beautiful parrots." Everyone looked up and saw the beautiful, colorful birds. "They are intelligent birds," Apari said, "but there are many people who buy parrots and do not care for them. Often people just keep a bird in a small cage and let them wither away. Animals are like humans. They need freedom and friends." The two children nodded in agreement. From above, the parrots waved, made funny faces, and sang. "There's a river back there. Let's rest there," Apari said. But then he warned: "Be careful! Dangers lurk everywhere."

Maka and Matz got off the ponies tired. Maki stretched out and yawned. He felt terrific. The humid, hot climate was similar to his home country. Maki was really happy because soon he would be going home. The two ponies trotted to the water because they were thirsty. Apari examined the area, while Maka and Matz spread a blanket and started looking for wood.

Suddenly the ponies roared like crazy, one stood on his hind legs, and Maki began to scream, so loud that the children were frightened. Then they saw Apari running to the ponies by the river. He had a stick in his hand and hit the water.

The children saw that a giant crocodile had the leg of one of the ponies in its mouth and tried to pull it in the water. He knew what he had to do. Apari jumped towards the crocodile and hit him between the eyes with a stick. The giant crocodile let go of the pony and swam away.

Everyone was shocked and helped the injured little horse. First, the wound had to be treated, but Apari immediately saw that the pony was only slightly injured. Matz quickly pulled bandages out of his small backpack. Yes, you should always have important things with you on hikes. Maka and Matz wrapped the leg of the pony. Everyone was happy that it could still run.

Whew, now they all had to sit down for a while. "That was close, but it went well," Matz said. Apari replied: "You see how dangerous it can be when you're unfamiliar or unprepared." Then he went into the lush green jungle to get plants, roots and water for everyone in the group.

Later in the evening, the injured pony was getting better. Then the events of the day were again discussed and evaluated. They were on the right track, and the city of Darwin was not too far. So everyone could fall asleep with new courage.

Groenlandia
(Din.)
Alaska
(EE.UU.)
CANADÁ
ESTADOS
UNIDOS
OCÉANO
BRASIL
PACÍFICO

Farewell to Australia

The next morning everyone was cheerful because it was only a day's march to their next destination. The attack of the dangerous crocodile was hopefully the last dangerous adventure that the children and animals had to experience on their way north. To protect the injured pony, no one should ride on him. Maka and Matz wanted to take turns walking and riding. Apari led them through the rainforest as if he had lived here for a long time.

Then they saw the city of Darwin on the horizon. Maka and Matz began to cheer. Maki, on the other hand, remained cool and rubbed his hands. He was doing well, but he was still a little homesick. And finally, there was Darwin, a city in northern Australia where more than a hundred thousand people lived. But even here, it was incredibly hot and people were still busy cleaning up. Maka and Matz were somewhat ashamed because it was their fault that the giant Tikitipua had stopped the world and everything was swirling.

The city already had big problems because there had often been heavy thunderstorms and hurricanes. Many houses were destroyed in the process. But the people were optimistic and friendly and greeted the small group. A young woman explained how to get to the harbor. Now it was not far.

When they reached it, they found a fisherman. They explained to him why they needed a boat. Of course, it should be a sailboat because Matz was a good sailor. "Hm," said the fisherman, who chewed a pipe in the corner of his mouth, "I need to see if we still have a boat that you can sail safely." Then he showed them a small sailboat. "Look at this one. It is old, but still well maintained and large enough for two children and a Maki. Is that good enough?" asked the friendly fisherman. "Yes!" Maka and Matz shouted at the same time. Maki squealed, "Never mind, I want to go home!"

The fisherman just grinned and went to a small boat shed to get sails, lines and life rings. Maka and Matz already looked at their new vessel.

At the same time, Apari took care of the two ponies. The fisherman came back and helped the children set sail. After a few minutes, the boat was seaworthy and could get going. They just had to load up the food and water. The fisherman looked into the distance and said, "The sun is shining and you have a light, good wind. But the clouds tell me that there might be a storm. In any case, I wish you all the best."

Maka and Matz were still excited and could hardly wait to set sail. But then they were sad. They had to say goodbye to Apari and their ponies. Apari promised to take care of the animals. Maka and Matz said goodbye to him with a hongi, and they shook hands with the fisherman. They hugged the ponies and promised to pick them up on the way back.

Then they both jumped into the boat. When they sat down, Apari handed Maki to them. Maka put him on her lap, while Matz hoisted the lines and set the sail. And off they went. The wind blew into their sails and they set off north towards Southeast Asia.

When they looked back, Apari, the fisherman and the two ponies stood there on the shore and waved. The four looked at them for a long time. Maka and Matz waved and shouted "Goodbye" until the small boat slowly disappeared on the horizon.

Now they were close to their goal of bringing Maki home. They were all really looking forward to it. But what would happen if there really were a storm? Would they be able to bring Maki home quickly and safely?

***

www.ingramcontent.com/pod-product-compliance
Lightning Source LLC
LaVergne TN
LVHW050558160826
845677LV00011B/2365

* 9 7 9 8 6 6 6 3 4 2 9 6 1 *